QUEEN VASHTI

By
Ariana Sanderson &
Tallmadge Swartzfager

2022

Queen Vashti.
Copyright © 2023 by Ariana Sanderson
All rights reserved.
First Printing, December 2022
Second Printing, April 2023

Published by Orange Broccoli Publishing; a division of Steamed Slices International.

Author(s): Ariana Sanderson, Tallmadge Swartsfager
Executive Editor: Tallmadge Swartzfager
Chief Editor: Ariana Sanderson
Copy Editors: Molly Mayo, Kaylin Fischer, Chiana Sanderson
Layout and Design: Rainey Gleich, Tallmadge Swartzfager
Art (in order of appearance): Lily Kreiger, Madeline Kleveter, Victor Baker

Song Lyrics: McConnell, Steve. "Adonai Yimloch", *We Delight*, 1996, track 10.

Contents.

Part 1 9

Part 2 17

Part 3 37

Part 4 61

Part 5 79

Part 6 91

Part 7 95

Part 8 99

Part 9 107

Part 10 113

Ending 127

View of the palace gardens 22
View of the commune 63
A time of reflection 125

Prologue

———

"ARRRR! Haman is here! Beware AAARGGH!!!"

Children screamed with laughter and terror, at the sudden intrusion of the scary reenactor. Some ran, others stood to fight the black clad invader. But one little boy stood apart from the thrills. He was old enough now to understand that "Haman" was just his Uncle Ben. And that the delicious Hamantaschens, bright costumes and food gifts, celebrating the Festival of Purim held a deeper dark underlying story ... one that almost wiped out his people, the Jews.

The story of Queen Esther and the Great Mordecai was told many times during this celebration. But his curiosity went further than what was retold. An intrigue encouraged by his Uncle's vague retelling of his remembrance of time spent there. "How he missed serving the Queen..."

Stealing away from the celebration, he passed his busy mother and slipped into his curious Uncle's chamber. Immediately, his eyes fell on paintings, papers, and fabrics strewn about the room in organized chaos. Such a strange man my Uncle is... This year he was going to find his answers.

Was that a scroll? A rather large one to include everyday business. Breathlessly, carefully undoing the string, he unraveled it, and was perplexed at the opening line of the scroll. All this time he assumed his uncle referred to serving Queen Esther... but in a bold title were the words:

QUEEN VASHTI

Part 1

"Call in Queen Vashti." The King refused to peel his eyes from the window. His breath came in shallow half-gasps and his head surged with emotions. He had forgotten the Greeks. His father had fretted over them, but he had forgotten them completely. They seemed the least of his problems, and so very far away — out of sight was out of mind to him and all of Persia. The Greeks were just goatherds and fishermen anyways, an insignificant people who dwelt in independent cities that fought amongst themselves more often than not. But now here they were, in the heart of Persia - and they had nearly annihilated Ahasuerus' army. The King did not want to admit it, but he was terrified. Shaken to his core. His hands shook, and when he realized, he gripped the window sill until his knuckles were white so nobody else would notice.

"CALL IN MY WIFE!" His arm whipped out and smashed a full goblet of wine across the table, sending the drink splattering across the floor like blood. Like the blood of the men that had spilled outside, of his soldiers who had been massacred. A few of his nobles turned their heads away, sickened by the sight of it.

His anger seeped into his speech. Feet scurried immediately. Queen Vashti was safely in the Northwest wing of the palace, almost a mile away from the King's windowed lookout, but as soon as the King spoke, three eunuchs, Tarshin, Harbonah, and Zethar, jumped to retrieve her. Half an hour later, she entered his chambers wearing a beautiful blue velvet evening dress, embroidered with stars up her bodice. The train of silk trailed past her feet and billowed behind her while Beanbean, her favorite eunuch, held the end of it. She looked annoyed to be there, until she followed Ahaseurus' gaze out of the window.

"Oh. Oh?" All of the words fell away from her. Vashti had always been sickened by the sight of blood. She had cried then fainted at the birth of her two oldest children, and every time she became pregnant with another, the dread filled her months in advance. This was no different.

"I don't know what to do," Ahasuerus admitted.

Thousands of Persians lay dead upon the field, horses and foot soldiers lying tangled in the wreck of war, the blood-soaked ground flowing in rivulets to the river. In the distance the Greek camp burned. Near at hand, wounded soldiers lay groaning and dying in the streets among those who had been slain by the valiant 10,000 of Greece. Some of the houses had been ransacked, doors broken in and windows shattered, pillaged by both Greek and Persian in the confusion and desperation of battle. Torn curtains fluttered mournfully in the weak breeze. The wails arose from the city as people and soldiers alike lamented the day and its great loss — so many men had died, they could not even be counted. Nor would they be, for the embarrassment was great enough without adding insult to injury. The weeping screams were a force stronger than the lonely wind, and it chilled the King to the core. His armies may have carried the field, but he could not consider this a victory. What if the Greeks returned? Cyrus might be dead, but very few of his soldiers had fallen. It terrified him.

The Greeks had been outnumbered two to one, yet had still been first to charge that day. It was not until Cyrus fell that Ahasuerus could convince his troops to advance against the Greeks — and even then, it was only to sneak behind them and despoil their camp. So many brave men fell against the scythed chariots alone — his own bodyguard, the best armed and trained cavalry in the world, had shied away from charging the Greek lines and winning eternal valor for themselves — they had done their duty to defend their King and kill Cyrus when he himself rode at the head of his men against the Persians, but after that they sat safely out of harm's way. With Cyrus dead, however, the Greeks quit the field, withdrawing in good order across the river, except for the valiant 10,000, who stood against the Persian army; and not only stood against it, but drove Ahasuerus' troops from the field and into the city. Few of his troops had not been thickly engaged in combat today — many of his men had lost friends and brothers this day.

"Huh." Vashti chewed on her nail, then examined her hand. She looked around at the room of wise men and eunuchs. "And what, the professional noise gallery doesn't have any commentary?"

"Vashti." The king's voice took on a warning edge as he looked out over his crowd of "wise men."

"The grape vine is silent, just this once?"

"My Queen, please, be serious." Zethar hissed, then returned to his stoic position. The Queen looked again out of the window. Taking a deep breath, she leaned both of her hands on Ahasuerus's shoulders. "How did this happen? Who is responsible for this?"

"It seems as though the Greeks have become a formidable enemy, your highness." A eunuch stepped forward, cowering low. He dared not look into her eyes. "It has been a while since we have joined our troops with Media, to keep them in line."

"How long would it have been for them to become this strong?" She gestured out of the window.

"My Queen, we're learning as much as we can about the situation, but these things take time."

Haman, a newer delegate, stepped forward and bowed while speaking to the Queen. His eyes never left her. "Under the circumstances, you'll have to understand how we're a bit confused ourselves."

"I'm not an idiot." She sneered, then leaned closer to her husband. "Who is he?"

"Haman, son of Hammedatha. He's new."

"That's Haman? I know his wife but I've never seen him before." She paused, squinting at him.

"He's kind of ugly. No wonder she doesn't mention him much."

"Vashti, please." The King pushed her hand off — then, after looking at her, pulled it back and kissed it gently.

They both turned back to look out for a few more seconds, taking a deep breath. A collective silence settled across the room.

Following a brief silence, Vashti gently grasped the King's face in her palm and turned it toward her. "Throw a party," Vashti whispered and turned her back on the entourage of advisors. "Your skin is pale, you look afraid. You can not let the people know you're afraid." She smiled pityingly at him.

"Rebuild, fortify, and celebrate. The people will forget, the so-called leaders you appoint will eventually forget, and you, my King," she paused and took both sides of his face in her hands, "You, too, will forget as you are busy with celebrations and preparations for such. Orontes is a good general. He will take care of the Greeks."

"My Queen," he gazed into her eyes and led her out of the room, "we are going to walk in the gardens." The delegates, who had been waiting for the King to make some kind of 'next move' decision, suddenly became invisible to him as they walked out of the room and through the hallways, down to the Queen's gardens.

~*~*~*~

"My king, you are wise," Vashti started when they reached the garden, passing through the ivy wrapped gates. She sat on a bench of stone and breathed in the beauty of the cultivated gardens. This was a part of her court. Her pride and joy.

"And you, my Queen, are beautiful."

"You have thousands in your armies and the smartest counselors at your disposal. This conflict with the Greeks will be only a small setback in the glory of your reign."

"Your words are as beautiful as you are, Vashti." Ahasuerus sighed, looking up at the countless stars.

The gardens and the West Court were the handy-work of the queen. All of the people within its walls loved her as much as she could imagine. They would sacrifice their lives for her, and that was exactly how she wanted it.

This life was perfect, and it was hers. Her mentally weak, impulsive King — her husband Ahasuerus — could never touch it.

Part 2

Smoke billowed from the kitchens like it had from the Greek camp at Cunaxa. Vashti would have worried about it, but she knew Estralita never burned chicken, so she turned from the window and in so doing turned her mind from her husband's feast to her own. Satraps and generals from all over the empire were gathering to discuss military and administrative matters with the king, and wine and dine with him. He kept them up late into the night with stories of his greatness and the proud lineage which was his, and have them up early for reviews of his Immortals. They would all be extremely occupied with those things — and they would all bring their wives. Vashti was charged to entertain and care for them while their husbands were otherwise engaged. Considering the largeness and opulence of Ahasuerus' palace, this could be a long time.

But, to her own concerns. Eunuchs and handmaidens were bustling all about — in the banquet hall, in the bedrooms, in the kitchens, in the gardens, in the pantries and storehouses and larders. There were wines and foods to gather, decorations to hang, beds to make, and a thousand different party favors to prepare for each of her guests, and Vashti had to oversee it all. Ahasuerus would undoubtedly open his treasure hoard nightly and bestow gifts upon his closest lieutenants and favored governors; Vashti would have to do the same with her visitors — she would be expected to.

The banquet hall was to be filled with tables — the eunuchs were bringing them in now, round cheeks rosy red with exertion — long, low tables surrounded by equally long and low couches mounded over with cushions. Up above great swaths of fabric were being hung between the colonnades of the vast vaulted ceiling — linen clothes of royal violet, great banners with the white and blue of Ahasuerus' house, purple from the West. Ornate tapestries hung for curtains from silver rods dividing off sections of the hall to facilitate the soirée — Vashti reveled in flitting from conversation to conversation, and loved storytelling in the evening. Garlands of flowers hung from the marble pillars — garlands and wreaths of jeweled flowers on silver and gold stems and vines with emerald leaves.

The couches and cushions were upholstered in the same cloths as hung above, on frames of acacia and sandalwood, and cypresses from Lebanon, gilded and studded in gold and silver, overworked in traceries of yet more silver and gold. Where the floor was not covered in rugs of violet and purple, the great marble pattern, alternating white and black stones, glistened from a recent polish. The maids had cleaned it this morning — now they were working along the walls, scrubbing and polishing the mosaics, which depicted scenes from the vast empire lands beyond the very edge of the world. The world of which Vashti was Queen. One-hundred and twenty-seven provinces. And all from here Vashti ruled it with her husband. And all to here, the peoples of the earth sent their wealth and treasures and people. She looked around at all her eunuchs and serving maids. Girls who looked like they had been weaned on lemons from India; pale Egyptians; swarthy daughters of the Hittites from Anatolia; blue-eyed Greeks from Thrace and beyond — many of them prisoners of war. This was all hers. They were all Vashti's.

At the far end of the room, through the open arch curtained with tapestries from the edge of the world, Vashti could see the outer garden with its fountain; and within the fountain grew a most recent pride and accomplishment, her blooming lotus flowers. Or, at least, hopefully "soon to be blooming."

Vashti had sent for them from India, after certain merchants from there said that the lotus was a particularly beautiful flower which ought to grace the gardens of the Queen of queens. So with utmost care and plenty of research, she had spent several months with her daughter cultivating and nurturing them until they finally grew from buds and seemed ready to bloom.

"My Queen!" One of the Queen's maidens hastened through the arch towards her, "It's the lotus, my lady. They're blooming."

The Queen, her gold dress shimmering in the sun, glided across the hall to see. Though it could be seen from the hall, it was a long way to the fountain, situated in the farthest part of the West garden. Vashti stuck to the colonnade, out of the sun. The conditions of Babylon differed slightly from the lotus' native home — more sun, dryer air, less rain. This made it hard for them to bloom, but under her watchful eye, and the consistent nurturing of her oldest daughter Nastaran, they finally began to see some progress. The palace gardeners would also take some credit for their successful cultivation, but it felt like Vashti and Nasta's perfect little secret. The hand-crafted rock waterfalls and gentle pools were meant to stay cool and flowing to keep the environment clean, while the gentle mists prevented them from growing too warm in the sun. After so much work, including the slight hitch of hiring a special craftsman to rebuild a better accommodating fountain — which took longer than she had wanted — Vashti hoped the merchants had not exaggerated.

As she reached the fountain, with the handmaiden Ilda behind her, Vashti found her daughter kneeling by the edge and reaching over towards the flowers, the long sleeves of her dress floating in the

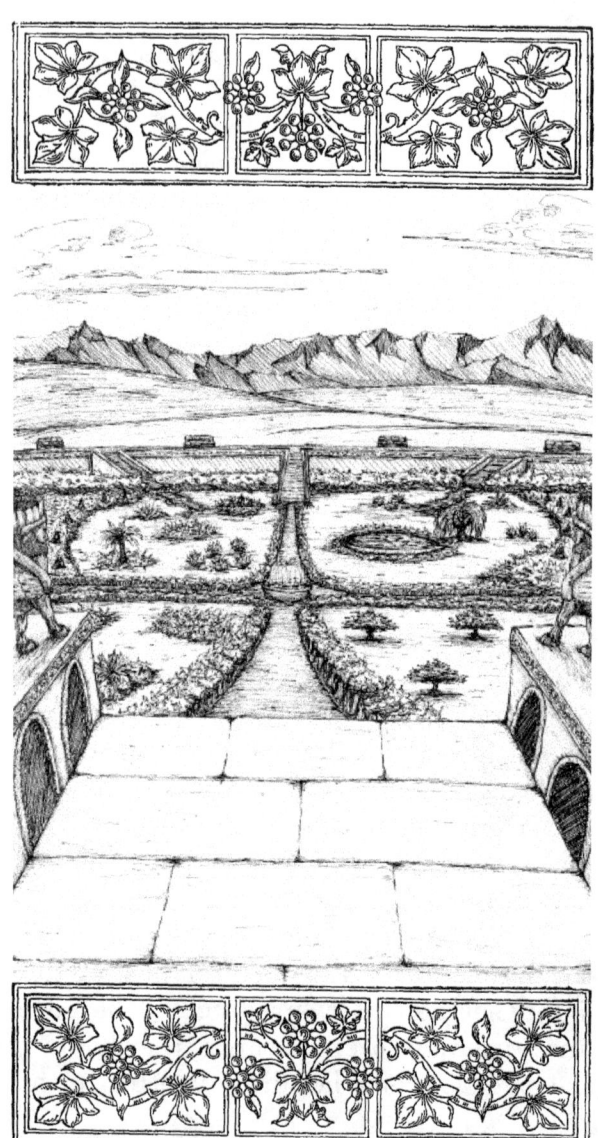

water. She was a picture of feminine grace and girlish innocence, smiling there, the water reflecting onto her face, her fingertips extended toward a lotus which was just out of reach. The lotus: a symbol of purity and new birth. It was fitting.

"My darling girl, your sleeves will be soaked." Vashti bent down next to her, sweeping her arms to collect the fabric from the water.

"It's worth it Mama." Nastaran pulled back her hands, shaking out the loose droplets with a light laugh. "Look!"

There in the water sat eight delicate little orbs, just starting to unravel and unfold into gentle color. The lotuses were on their way to full bloom.

Vashti sighed and sat down on the edge of the fountain as she admired the fruit of their labors.

"I'm sure more will bloom soon," Nastaran turned to look at her mother, "Isn't it exciting? Isn't it beautiful, mama?"

"By the time of the banquet, we'll be able to bring our guests to the gardens and show them this, the waterfalls and the flowers. It would be lovely to hold a reception out here. Just picture it. The delicate foods, a few couches for after dinner lounging, and..."

All day mother and daughter planned how they would exhibit the gardens to their guests, discussing what plants were better to show in the morning or evening. Some rearrangements they had made immediately. Others they planned out in their heads. Vashti finally had the gardens set up the way she wanted them. On the outer walls and around all the fountains and waterfalls, the courtyard would be full of flowers, and in the center of it all, like a crowning jewel, at least thirty lotus flowers bobbing gently with the wind and gently rushing waters. She would have a score of candles illuminating the edge of the pool. It would be the main attraction. Of all the things the King and his Queen took pride in, these gardens were supreme. Who but the mightiest King had the security and wealth to enjoy such beauty and smell the roses? And what Queen would not enjoy such fruit from the works of her hand and heart.

As the evening descended, Vashti sent Nastaran to join her younger siblings until she finished preparations for the banquet. Everything was still a hustle and a bustle, but things were going smoothly. Beanbean was beside her now, silent and watchful as a cat.

"While I have you," said the Queen, "go tell my husband I have completed my preparations, and that I wish him to come and see." Beanbean bowed and slipped away. A smile tugged at the corners of her mouth. Vashti draped herself in a chair and turned to look at the newest tapestry in her palace, which hung in a place of preeminence. It depicted the death of the pretender Cyrus at the Battle of Cunaxa, the burning of the Greek camp and the pillaging of their army. For certain, it was embellished from the reality of the day, but it painted her husband in a favorable light — and if all these wives were convinced Ahasuerus was a hero, their husbands would likely soon believe it too. It would also make her a hero in her husband's eyes.

But to make *her* eyes happy, and more importantly her heart, Nastaran came around the outside of the archway, dressed in what would be her evening attire. Purple and gold with sleeves that billowed out like her mothers and clasped at the wrist. And of course the royal princess' crown, that was uncomfortable but pretty enough for Nasta to grit her teeth and deal with. She came to her mother's side, grinning as she looked at the bobbing lotus flowers, dancing on the water. Vashti stroked her child's hair, kissing the top of her head affectionately.

"We did it! We've successfully gone from cultivating rosemary and lavender plants to lotuses!" The eight-year-old beamed up at her mother.

"And you have grown from wearing rosemary and vine wreaths to the crown of a princess."

Vashti smiled, dreaming of the day she would see the crown placed on her daughter's head, determined that she would be there to commission the royal portraits when her daughter was to be married. The gold crown, with the symbols of Persia's greatness wrapped around it, and the pearls of Persia dangling from the bottom, would fit her beautifully when it was her time. Vashti could only wait.

She leaned on her daughter's head, closing her eyes as she remembered when Nastaran was four years old and had come into her quarters with handfuls of rosemary that she had ripped from the garden. She had cried because her nursemaid scolded her for killing the plants, but instead of chastising her as well, Vashti twisted them into a crown, substituting the missing space with ivy that had overgrown her balcony, and placed the wreath on her daughter's head. *One day the kingdom will be in your hands and you will be old enough for a real crown, but for now you'll have to wear this one.*

Nastaran looked at her mother with eyes that twinkled like stars, as big as the moon. Her mother was not only the Queen in her eyes, but the very cultivator of life. During every available second of the day, she trailed alongside Vashti, soaking up everything. Nastaran, princess of Persia, second in line to the throne, was in many ways her mother's double. The gardens wove them together as the vines on palace walls, and when Nastaran became Queen, she would continue the legacy by cultivating beautiful gardens of her own. Vashti and Nastaran walked together with linked arms silently hoping that Ahasuerus would join them, so their entire family could be together for even just a little while. Bahar and Ayena, the two youngest, rolled and kicked a wooden ball back and forth under the weeping willow trees. Vashti sat on a stone bench, watching the nursemaids trip after them to ensure they did not fall. Nastaran knelt by the water, gazing at the lotuses. The only people that seemed to be missing were Ahasuerus and…

"My Queen." Beanbean returned, faster than she had expected, but…alone. "The King…ahh," he started.

"Mama!" Vashti's firstborn son, Arash, came from behind Beanbean. He made a beeline for the pool, rushing over to look at the gentle lotus flowers that his mother and sister had been nurturing for months. "They're so awesome. Can I touch one?"

"No, Arash! I don't want you to soak your clothing. We have the banquets tonight!"

With child-like defiance, he jumped in anyway, splashing and soaking his clothes immediately.

Nastaran squealed when the water splashed onto her face, and scrambled up, hiding behind her mother.

"Nasta, get in! These petals look even softer up close!"

"Ah, Arash, be careful not to step on any of the vines. They grow on the bottom of the pool."

"I'm being careful, mama." He waded, the water rising up to his chest, as he got closer to the cluster. "Nasta!"

Nastaran looked at her mother, then back at Arash, back and forth. "Nastaran, you're going to be late to the banquet if you get in that water."

"I have enough time before sundown!" Nastaran quickly slid out of her sandals and into the pool, bouncing on her toes to keep her chin above water as she waded out to meet her brother.

"Nasta!" Vashti walked to the edge, then sighed, turning back to Beanbean. "Is her nursemaid nearby?"

"Yes, I believe so. I can retrieve her. But..."

"Where's Ahasuerus?"

He hesitated, rolling back and forth on his heels for a second. He stepped closer and lowered his voice. "The King," he whispered so that only his lady could hear, "has bid me tell you he is much too busy with his own preparations ... and he bids you," the eunuch continued slowly, "make sure your own are complete."

Vashti's eyes widened and her nostrils flared, provoking Beanbean to take a step back, bowing his head in a gesture that said, "I am just the messenger." *So, he was too busy with his own preparations, was he? She ought to make sure her own were complete, ought she?* Angrily, she strode back into the great hall again. The servants, including her eunuchs and maids were still decorating, but froze in their places as she entered. "Bigthan, Teresh!" she barked, "take that tapestry down," she whipped her hand out, pointing an accusatory finger at the repulse of the Greeks, "and roll it up in a corner! Let the mice and moths get at it — or cut it up into rugs and give it to the poor!" They bowed and hastened to obey. Ahasuerus had better enjoy his banquet. She spun around at the sound of her children's laughter, which now mildly annoyed her.

"Nastaran, Arash. Out of the lotus pool. Now."

~*~*~*~

How long could men drink and jest? After the first hundred days, Vashti caught her second wind and stopped complaining — these past eighty nights had been better than the first eighty! At this point, the assembly of women had worked through most of their differences, addressed their problems, and learned to all love each other as sisters. Attrition had broken down their façades, and now the tears were shared and genuine, the laughter was hearty and long, and the stories in the evening were well told and from the heart. Ilda, Vashti's favorite serving girl, a blonde-haired and blue-eyed maiden from far beyond Greece and north of Scythia, was busy writing down the tales, though her Persian was still rather poor in all forms. Frequently, several of the older women took time to teach her new words and help her along. Vashti relished the privilege of serving as matriarch to a thousand sisters and mothers; a position both of power and of love. She was obeyed and adored. She specially regarded these elderly women who had comforted her through morning sickness!

She could almost forget that Ahasuerus, after insulting her, had ignored her this whole time. In a moment of magnanimity, when the banquet had turned into a sisterhood, she had brought the tapestry of Cunaxa back out and hung it up for all to see. The woman had admired it and "oohed" and "awed" at the depiction of Ahasuerus cutting down Cyrus the Pretender in combat. Vashti had sent a private message to her husband, a word only for his ear, inviting him to visit her to see the exceptional tapestry she commissioned — but he never sent a word back. After holding her peace for too long, she ordered the tapestry taken out again and burned. As all the women stared at the scene with wide eyes and silent mouths, she revealed the truth about how the King slighted her in the matter of the tapestry and the banquet preparations, and all that really happened at the battle, how the King stood afar off and surveyed the scene helplessly until she arrived, and how he ignored her requests for his presence. As she recalled the memory, her eyes clouded and her attention drifted...

"Are you alright, *ak vean ku'ear?*" spoke a soft voice in her ear.

Vashti focused her glare upon Ilda. The girl cowered ever so slightly, but quickly the Queen softened her gaze. Ilda's Persian was still sufficiently poor that she said strange and funny things like *ak vean ku'ear* instead of "My Lady."

"Yes, Ilda," the Queen said, "thank you. Go check on my children. I was hard on them earlier. Please let me know they're alright." Ilda nodded, smiled, and slipped away. To Vashti, it felt like she spent more time with her children over the past months than she had in time gone by, but it was not enough, and one of her maidens was always checking on them. It never felt like enough time and before she knew it, her dear, little lotus flowers would blossom into kings and queens. The laughter and chatter that filled the room, along with Ilda's interruption served to dispel the clouds of the black mood settling on Vashti. Almost.

Just then Beanbean was at her elbow, leaning down to whisper in her ear. "Harbonah is here — from the king."

Vashti turned, knowing full well that Harbonah had not waited at the door, but had followed Beanbean: the king's eunuchs out-ranked all of her own, just as Ahasuerus out-ranked her — and how he loved to lord it over her! There he was, the spider, with six others.

"Queen Vashti," the spider began to weave his web of words, "King Ahasuerus bids you come before him in the presence of all his guests, and he bids you wear your royal crown, for he says it suits the beauty of your face well. Also he desires you to wear the gown you wore when Cyrus the Pretender perished at Cunaxa, for he says it suits you well, and he desires to display the unsurpassed beauty of his Queen before all, for you are more beautiful than Aphrodite and Artemis of Greece."

The noise of the hall reduced to a murmur, for all had heard Harbonah's proclamation and recalled the story Vashti shared with them and how disgraced she was. Vashti recalled also. Turning to face her guests and friends, she declared, "See. I am more beautiful than any Psyche or Helen of Greece, than any mortal, hero, or goddess! So says my husband, though he has never set a foot in Achaia, nor crossed the Hellespont! He has been too busy with his banquet to make war — mighty Persia, tied down in drinking and feasting and unable to conquer these sea-faring goatherds! — and too busy to find time for his wife, without whom he would be nothing. Who stood beside him at the siege of Babylon? Who counseled and consoled him at the Battle of Cunaxa? He remembers my beauty so well, but he cannot remember to make time for his own wife? I do indeed have a royal crown upon my head.

"You," she turned sharply upon Harbonah, "go tell my husband, the King, that I will not be coming down to his hall. I am the Queen, and I am engaged with my own guests. Perhaps when he is less busy, and I myself can find the time, we two can meet and discuss whatever pressing business he might presume to interrupt my banquet for. Go, tell him that, Harbonah." Before the king's eunuchs had left the hall she added to her ladies loud enough for the messengers to hear, "I, at least, will deign to answer a simple request." The eunuchs turned at the door. "What is it the Jews say?" Vashti pondered aloud, casting a glance at them, "Open rebuke is better than hidden love?"

Without a word, the King's eunuch's met her gaze and then passed through the door.

"I fear, my Queen, you may suffer the king's wrath for this," Beanbean whispered in her ear again as the banquet returned to its constant hum of conversation.

"I do not fear the king's wrath," she hissed bitterly.

Part 3

The banquet continued, with the women of the court laughing and giggling, fantasizing about how it would appear if they defied their husbands in this way. But, as the King's eunuchs filed out, Vashti was left with a sudden feeling of worry. Her hand covered her stomach, as she thought of the little life growing inside of her. She fretted for her baby's future … but, no, the eunuchs had told her that he was ridiculously drunk. Ahasuerus would never remember. He would hardly notice… Vashti brushed off the feeling and went on with her evening.

Her closest friend, Zeresh, glided over to her table, grinning. "All hail Queen Vashti, the only queen worthy of respect." She raised her glass and all across the hall, women did the same, cheering for Vashti's win against her husband. Vashti politely nodded and everyone went back to their conversations. Zeresh took the seat to Vashti's right, sighing contentedly.

"Haman keeps asking me to attend his late night rendezvous with his friends. All he does at them is boast about his wealth and position. Maybe next time, I'll say no."

"You should." Vashti sipped her drink. "That sounds boring and dull."

"Oh trust me, it is."

Conversation babbled on for quite a while, leading Vashti to grow weary. She was determined to enjoy this night though.

An hour later, Beanbean showed up running. The evening was winding down, with most of the women lounging across pillows and couches. He stumbled toward her, panting. After whispering hurriedly to the Queen, instantaneous fear filled her face. She could not look at his face, because then she would know it was true.

"The King said what?"

The room became audibly quiet.

"My Queen, you're...being sent away."

Part 3.

~*~*~*~

Vashti hurried down the hallways toward her King, her shimmering, golden gown flowing behind her, billowing sleeves clasped around her wrists. Zeresh followed close behind with her silk, silver gown complementing the shine of her friend's, much like the sun and the moon.

"He's putting you away?"

"They say he's divorcing me. Divorcing. Me. Why? And what about the children? Oh, my children", she wailed.

Zeresh peeled off, running down a narrow corridor to the left, and was immediately replaced with Beanbean.

Zethar, the eunuch who was favored by the Queen, also joined them in their dash to the King.

"Who gave him that idea? He didn't think of that by himself. He wouldn't. Would he?" She slowed for a moment, bracing her hand against her stomach again. Beanbean looked to Zethar silently deciding who would answer.

"It was Memuchan, your highness."

Vashti sighed as a short-lived relief washed over her: it was not Ahasuerus' idea. Her eunuchs let out a breath, knowing that if her emotions were more intense, she would spiral and the blame would soon shift to them.

"He's always having problems with his wife," Beanbean continued, anxiously side-eying Zethar.

"She's smarter than he is and it bothers him. He genuinely believes the gods gave him a better sense of humor and more knowledge simply because he's a man."

He rolled his eyes and laughed.

They resumed their quick stride down the hallway.

Coming quickly upon her quarters, they rounded the corner to find everything being uplifted and moved. Eunuchs were everywhere and none of them would look at her. Trumpets blasted from the bottom of the stairs, startling Vashti. She rushed to the balcony overlooking the entrance to this wing of the palace, just as the courtier read the decree with a voice loud enough for the whole wing to hear:

"Let it be written in the laws of Persia and Media, which cannot be repealed, by order of King Ahasuerus, who rules over 127 provinces, in the third year of his reign, that the former Queen Vashti is never again to enter the presence of King

Ahasuerus. Also let the King give her royal position to someone else who is better than she. May this teach the women of our great nation to respect their husbands."

A deep guttural scream erupted from Vashti's throat, as she slowly sank to her knees. Two eunuchs appeared on either side of her, pushing Beanbean and Zethar out of the way, poised to drag her away to join the rest of her belongings. Her youngest two children started crying, clinging onto each other while their mother was taken away in front of them.

"Wait! Wait. My children. I have to say goodbye to my children."

She looked in the eunuch's eyes to plead with them, and only then recognized it was Patrichan and Anderru; two eunuchs she knew. They looked at each other and released her arms, letting her descend to the ground. Anderru stepped back for a second to let them come to her and after a few heartbeats, Patcrichan did the same.

"Please. Please just let me say goodbye," she pleaded.

Both averted their eyes from her, So she grasped the opportunity to go and ran to her dear ones, almost tripping on her skirts.

"Ayena, Bahar, come to me."

The two little things ran to her and fell into her arms, sobbing. She felt like her world was being torn away from her so suddenly that her lungs felt like they were collapsing and it was hard to breathe. They were so young. Only three and five. She would never get the chance to see them grow.

"Listen to me. Listen to me carefully. Follow the instructions of your brother. Arash will know what to do. Listen to Arash and Nastaran. Stay away from your father when he's angry."

She was gasping for air now, and there was no difference between crying and drinking air.

"Mama?"

Arash was standing in the doorway, with his sister hiding behind him. Nastaran was unashamedly sobbing. Her entire face had fallen and she trembled, gripping onto her brother's sleeve."Mama, what's happening?"

"I have to go away, my darling, I'm sorry. I am so sorry." Nastaran moved to run towards her, but Arash pulled her back, watching the eunuchs. Patrichan and Anderru turned their backs, only then giving the signal that it was okay to approach her. Nasta was on her in a flash, shaking and sobbing against her mother's side. Vashti looked pointedly, "keep your siblings safe."

"Mama, I'm sorry I drenched my clothes." Arash hiccuped, wiping his face with his arm. "I'm sorry I got in the pool and—" Another hiccup interrupted him. "And dragged Nastaran to — to join me. I'm sorry."

"That's not your fault. None of this is your fault, my treasure. Never think that."

She held his forehead against hers, taking a moment to breathe for just a second, possibly the last time she would be held by all of her children. Then she had to let herself be dragged by the eunuchs. Bahar fled from the room.

"No! You can't take her! She's the Queen! And she's my mom!" Arash's voice cracked, and Vashti's heart shattered against that stone, cold floor. Ten-year-old Arash, still a boy, pulled on the eunuch's arm, trying to overpower him. The eunuch could not look the boy in the eyes. Tears streamed down his chubby cheeks, and he hiccuped, voice wavering and breaking as he pulled and beat on the arms of the men taking his mother away. He knew she would most likely not be put into exile, as were most people who fell into the dangerous bad graces of his father. The King of Persia knew no mercy.

Out of the corner of her eye, Vashti saw a streak of blonde hair disappearing into the darkness of the palace passageways. "Please, don't make this harder than it needs to be. I'll send you a letter, from wherever I am sent. You will hear from me again. I promise." She hugged Arash and Nastaran again, holding them close and hard. Ayena held onto the edge of her dresses as tight as she could. It felt like her life was being sucked away from her so quickly.

The two eunuchs dragged her down hallway after hallway, until she began to get dizzy. "I will be able to write, right? My children will hear from me."

Patrichan and Anderru glanced at each other. Anderru sucked his teeth and shook his head. "Not according to the King's wishes."

"Why? He just wants me gone, right? What does *'gone'* mean exactly? Will I see them again?"

Both grew silent, instead choosing to listen to her screams transition from

Part 3. 45

confusion to panic as they echoed off the high ceilings. They finally stopped outside, on a desolate part of the courtyard. Four more eunuchs were waiting for them. One leaned upon the great curved blade of a scimitar.

Dread filled Vashti's stomach, and she started screaming harder, kicking and fighting to get away from them, but the eunuchs held her mightily. It was a sickening death march. As her sandals fell from her feet, leaving her to scramble backwards, two men, who each individually doubled her weight, dragged her forward.

The two knocked her down to her knees and pinned her arms behind her, stepping on her shoulders so she could not move. Her cries were becoming more hysterical now, and her long wails continued to permeate the building.

"Stop! WAIT! In the name of the King, stop!" A pleading scream announced the hasty arrival of the Queen's friend, and her handmaiden. Zeresh and Ilda came around the corner, Ilda immediately throwing herself between Vashti and the executioner. The shadow of the scimitar loomed over both of their heads poised to strike both of them down in an instant.

"Don't do it. Please!" The faithful girl pleaded, quaking and trembling with her arms raised above her head. The eunuch hesitated.

"Do you dare lay hands on the Queen of Persia? Your Queen?" Zeresh pulled her friend to her feet, holding her as she leaned for support. Vashti was still crying and shaking slightly, but with the support of Zeresh, she regained a bit of her composure.

"The King's decree removed her from the palace and thus we have been sent by one of his right hand to execute her," responded the executioner.

"The King's right hand does not correctly demonstrate the will of the King. I can assure you that he does not want her dead," demanded the loyal friend.

"Orders are orders." He lifted the scimitar again.

"NO!" Both women cowered into each other. "What if I could offer a compromise? That way all of us leave happy. And alive."

Vashti held onto Zeresh's hand, and together balanced out the shaking in the other. Usually it was Vashti using her words to get them out of a particularly difficult situation, but when the time had come, Zeresh proved herself able to do the same for her dear friend.

"What if…"

~*~*~*~

Ilda quickly packed as many of the Queen's dresses into a trunk as she could. As soon as the bags were packed, Beanbean carried the trunks out to the carriages that were available.

Another handmaiden quickly brought up a basket of food from the kitchen. "My Queen, you must not delay. There is no time for such things. We must go."

Ilda stopped and looked at her. "You're going?"

"Yes," the other handmaiden whispered, "you're not?"

"Well I… I wasn't sure."

"Come with us, please," another maiden came up behind her, clasping both of her hands.

"Oh well I, I'm not sure. I — This is all so sudden."

"It's either this or explain to her children where their mother disappeared, while also keeping them quiet for the king."

"And the Queen is going to need a nursemaid for when she has the baby."

She waited for a moment, and the Queen was on the edge of breaking down again. Ilda looked at her once, and then again.

"Oh, stars. All right."

The maidens quietly shared their excitement, and Ilda ran from the room to collect her few belongings from the maidens' quarters.

One maid wrapped Vashti in a dark heavy cloak and they all worked together to whisk her away into the wagon. A blanket covered her head, and she sat silent for a few seconds.

As the blanket was ripped off, she shrank back, until she saw it was Zeresh.

"Be strong, friend." Zeresh gently squeezed her friend's injured shoulders and pressed into her hand a necklace set identical to the very one around her dear friend's neck. A rich gift from years past, when they were both young and enjoying the new riches of the palace together.

Vashti was wrapped in a dark evening cloak and whisked out from the palace so quickly, it left her head spinning. She kept thinking about Arash's face, and how desperately Nastaran and Ayeda had clung to her dresses.

As the wagon pulled away, Vashti watched Zeresh slit the throat of a lamb, letting its blood spill out on the courtyard floor, in the same place she would have lain dead if Zeresh had not stepped in to save her. At the ripe age of twenty-five, Vashti felt as if she had been impaled with a sword that cut three ways, piercing every part of her soul. Her children would cry, and they would be told to act as if their mother did not exist. And eventually, the palace would heal and it would be like she had never been there. Her gardens would forget she cultivated them, and her King, weak and stupid as he was, would forget he ever loved her. That is, assuming he ever loved her in the first place.

Traveling away from the palace for the last time felt like the longest and most painful journey of her life. She felt numb. There were too many tumultuous emotions and devastating feelings to experience at the same time, so she shut herself down.

Days passed and they still continued to travel. Many of her palace belongings were sold right in front of her eyes as they passed through random towns, but she could not bring herself to care.

Eventually, they arrived at a secluded compound. Ilda, lying next to her in the wagon, told her that when they crossed into Arabia, and when she peeked out through the curtains and saw the mountains, the beauty made Vashti....

Angry. It should not be beautiful. There should be no sloping hills and soft grass in a place of banishment. It should not be welcoming and the people here should not have been so inviting and kind.

Six women came to greet her, all decked out in dark dresses and head coverings. They spoke softly, even though the gentleness of their voices came to Vashti only as muffled noise. They led her to an open room and laid her in a soft bed. It should not be like this. She should be in a place that mirrored the state of her mind. A dark prison with disgusting guards and a hard floor to sleep on. Vashti refused to eat
when they brought her warm bread and sweet smelling teas. She would not bathe. She would not explore her new home. She just laid in bed, as the world passed by her. Her eunuchs carried the rest of her belongings in, and her seven maids set everything up, making the room look

presentable, even though it was nothing when compared to the stature of her previous home. Zethar even brought flowers and incense, but it only catapulted Vashti out of her current reality and into the caverns of her mind.

The first day she saw the blue of the sky, Beanbean came into her room and sat there for a while, perched on one of her Persian lounging pillows, watching her sulk. He ordered the women to leave her a little food, and a glass of water, then to leave. When she rubbed her eyes and actually looked at him, he had a smile on his face that reminded her of childhood mischief.

~*~*~*~

"There she is. The future Queen of Persia." Young Beanbean, given into the imperial service by his father as a sacrifice for the advancement of his family, sympathized immediately with young Vashti, future Queen, also bitter at the part she had to play in the destiny of her house. His real name was forgotten - his father had taken it back when they castrated him.

"My father said I'm not supposed to befriend eunuchs."

"Is your father the Queen of Persia?"

She looked at him in shock and protested, "You can't say that."

"What are they gonna do to me? Make me a eunuch?"

Against her will, it made her smile. Beanbean was supposed to be a gift to her, but instead he was sent away for many long years. But then, the moment Vashti entered Ahasuerus' court, two things happened. She realized that she did not like him, and she again met Beanbean. He was a soldier, and wore one of those ridiculous looking helmets that sat like enormous beans on top of their heads. They were happy to see each other, but his attitude was far too casual.

"Beans, you are still my servant. You report to me."

"Of course, your highness." He rolled his eyes, but still smiled.

She watched him warily for a minute, chewing on a date. "Are there particular tea leaves that will make my skin clear?"

Little by little, she began to trust him, and become his friend — keeping, however, the power difference intact.

Beanbean was by her side at the birth of her second child. When she delivered a girl, and Ahasuerus, in his disappointment, began drinking instead of coming to visit them, Beanbean was there, congratulating her for surviving the birth. Nastaran had been a hard one to pass, and she almost did not make it, but Beanbean remained by her side.

"There she is...," he said, very encouragingly wiping the sweat from her forehead and her neck. "The Queen of Persia."

~*~*~*~

"There she is. The Queen of Persia. Well, maybe not after this."

Vashti slowly ran a hand through her disheveled hair. The faint sound of singing came from the hallway, a song that sounded vaguely familiar. Beanbean bustled about, opening the window sash, talking about something irrelevant and annoying. Vashti's attention drifted away and her mind followed the sound of music coming from the open doorway.

> Though the sun may one day shine no more,
> though the waves may stop their race to the shore,
> though the birds of the air may no longer sing,
> though the winter fails to be followed by spring.
> Adonai yimloch l'olam vaed...

The music faded out as Beanbean kicked the door closed, trying to get her to focus.

She shook her head, focusing back on Beanbean's words. "After what?"

"You might be interested to know," he waved a letter in front of her, and she stood up.

"What's that?"

"A letter from Arash."

Vashti gasped, covering her mouth with both hands. With a flick of the wrist, Beanbean revealed not one letter, but two.

"And Zeresh. I have a feeling you'll like Arash's letter a bit more."

"Did you read them?" She stumbled out of bed, wrapping her nearest robe around her body. "Are they okay? What is Ahasuerus doing? Has he killed himself?"

"No. They are right as rain, I'm sure. He is not dead."

Vashti had already stopped listening to Beanbean and gently snatched Arash's letter from his hand. Opening it hastily, she read it, a smile spreading across her face. Suddenly her expression transformed from relief to...confused anger.

Mama,

I don't know where you've gone or why they've taken you, but I promise to bring you back home. There are so many women around the palace. Not the people you were friends with. These women are from all across the provinces. Most are not much older than I am. They all swarm around, talking about being pretty and Pedar¹. Always, the King of Persia they speak of. They talk about it around me, like I'm a wallflower. Invisible to them. I'm absolutely sure none of them know he is my father. It has been only two weeks, but we saw Pedar once, the morning after you left. He looked angry at me, like it was my fault you were gone. I protected Nastaran, though. Nasta and Ayena, and Bahar.

Do you have a name for the baby? When is the baby coming? I hope you are safe, maman. None of these women in the palace will ever be able to replace you.

*Your son and firstborn,
Arash.*

"My son, my joy." She pressed the letter to her chest, and enjoyed the feeling for a moment, even if it brought sadness Then the dots started connecting. "Bean? What did my child mean when he said there are young women in the palace? Who would come to replace me?"

Silently, he handed her the letter from Zeresh.

---

[1] A formal Persian address for "Father."

There was a country-wide search for a new Queen. Ahasuerus had dispatched another decree, and sent out messengers across all 127 of his provinces, which summoned all of the beautiful virgins to the palace. Vashti sat heavily on the bed, causing the frame to creak in protest. She scanned the letters two, three and four times. Each time made her more nauseous, until she started crying and could not stop.

"Are you ready to eat now?"

"What good is eating?" She wailed, burying her face in her hands. Beanbean rolled his eyes.

"You need your strength to lead. More than this, you need to resolve to do better not for yourself," he paused, considering, "but for others — in the way you failed as Queen of Persia. That might prove to yourself that you are better than Ahasuerus. But that's the root of the problem, now isn't it?"

"He's throwing a country-wide search to build a harem and that's your first thought?"

"Yes. You were raised to be a Queen. Whenever you're ready, the position will be waiting for you. You just have to make the decision for yourself to take on that role."

"I have changed my mind!" She yelled, then sat up straight. "Don't say his name here at all. Don't say it."

"With all due respect, majesty, I'm not going to do that."

"You have to."

"Acting like he doesn't exist won't help your current situation at all."

Beanbean walked to the door, taking the pot of cold tea with him. "Think about it, Queen. That position starts by cleaning yourself up and eating breakfast."

He left Vashti to her own thoughts. Sullenly, she scanned the room, which was smaller than what she was accustomed to, but open and spacious. *Become Queen of a place like this? What was the point?*

Her mind wandered to the child she was carrying — Ahasuerus' fifth child. *Would she be a strong leader for that child? A loving mother? If it was a boy, would they let the child stay in the compound or send him back to his father? What kind of life would there be for such a child?*

After another week of laying in her bed and doing the little things, opening her windows, sweeping the floor, eating, another letter came. From Nastaran.

Mama,

I was told you weren't dead. But, Mama, I thought you were dead. I saw the courtyard covered in blood. It was such a relief to hear. Why can't you come back? Why did father send you away? The night they took you away, they burned the garden. Ayena wept and I held her tight. I protected her and Bahar, just like you told me to. But I started crying too. I think the water saved all of the lotus flowers. They're the only thing that survived. Hannaiah came back from wherever you are. She left again, and said she would bring you my letter. Father is trying to replace you as quickly as he can. I don't know why he sent you away. His advisors are scared of him. They are trying to replace you too. Father must have asked

them to find a new Queen. I don't want a new queen — I want you home. The morning after they took you away he searched for you. I don't know why. He went through your rooms, and through the gardens. Father scares me, Mama. Can you come home and fix everything? He found me at the lotus pools, surrounded by the burnt ashes of the West Wing hall, and became angry with me. When father tried to grab me, Arash came between and protected me just like you told him. We spent the rest of the day in his room. I promise to keep the lotuses glowing for you. And to take care of Bahar and Ayena like you took care of me. I love you mother, for you are *the one who made me a true Queen. Please at least tell me you're alive. I miss you Mama.*

Nastaran

When she finished reading the letter, Vashti clutched it close to her chest, sobbing until she grew exhausted. Hours later she awoke with renewed purpose. Vashti promised herself — no — promised her children that she would talk to someone tomorrow. Someone outside of Beans and Zethar, her only contacts to this point. Because as much as she hated hearing the truth, her eunuch was correct. She had to get her life back on track.

PART 4

For the first time since her arrival, Vashti departed her room and decided to be a little bit better for herself. Immediately, she was met by a young, friendly woman with long curly black hair, who was waiting outside her door. Startled, Vashti jumped back a bit. The girl giggled, apologized and introduced herself as Chaya, a member of the religious community there. While she was not exactly a priestess, she was something akin to that; they called themselves "Daughters of Jephthah," whatever that meant — something to do with a vow of chastity to their God. They all referred to and considered each other "Sisters". The connection she had with the sisters was close-knit, like family. Or so she said. Either way, this young girl gave her a full tour of the compound, including the kitchens, the hills and valleys outside, the lodgings, the sanctuary, and the cellars where they stored their food for winter.

"We even have a library of ancient texts. Outside of these walls, I wouldn't have been taught to read." Vashti raised her eyebrows. It was a room the same size as a bedroom, but completely lined with books and maps along the walls.

Chaya introduced the woods as "the place I go to pray," and deep within that resonated with Vashti. There were no altars or statues in the woods, but this girl came here, by herself, to worship.

"I really hate this place. Its beauty infuriates me," Vashti grumbled. They paused and sat outside, watching the compound from a nearby hill. Vashti laid out on the grass exhausted and winded from walking up and down and up and down stairs and hills. Energized by the walking, the unborn baby in her 7-months-pregnant belly kicked as she settled into the grass, then stilled. Vashti stared at the tree-line behind the commune, purposefully taking deep breaths to steady herself, fighting the dizziness and nausea.

"How many months?" Chaya pointed to her stomach.

"What's in a month?" Vashti answered. "I'm counting down the days."

Chaya nodded and looked away.

"Anyway, I cannot comprehend how a place of banishment could feel so peaceful and beautiful."

Vashti looked at the girl, truly seeing her for a second. She had a round face, her skin tone only a little paler than her own. Across Chaya's nose and cheeks was a smattering of freckles, which she had not noticed before. Her freckles were the same color of her almond-shaped hazel eyes. So not only was she pretty, she was at peace.

"You like it here?"

Chaya considered for a second before answering. "It's hard for me to be here sometimes. I miss the family I used to have."

The Queen hummed in response, chewing the inside of her lip, failing to push the thoughts of her agonized children from her mind. She had tried and tried to push their terrified screams from her mind, but she could not stop their voices from creeping into her head at night. The country was so quiet, with nothing to buffer the sound.

"Why then are you here?"

"I'm afraid that's a long story." Chaya opened her mouth like she was going to speak, but stopped. "My family was taken by the Babylonians. Before the attack of the Persians, my father sent my sisters and I away while he and my brothers stayed to fight. We haven't heard from them since. For a while my mother and sisters and I lived in the small town down the road, but when my older sister came of age, we felt safer in the sisterhood. In time, my sisters left, but my mother refused leaving, so I stayed. She died a few months after my sisters left. Still, I feel... safe here."

Vashti answered with silence. She did not want to feel safe here.

"I came here when I was about eleven, and it just felt like home to me, even though I'd been without a home for quite some time. I hope that is soon the case for you."

"I guess we'll see." Vashti responded with a tone that was more sarcastic than Chaya was accustomed to.

Within moments, Vashti's frosty demeanor started to warm. Moving forward she would go to Chaya instead of her handmaidens to request tea to ease her pregnancy sores and swellings. Most of her maidservants had blended into the culture of the commune and would only come around occasionally to make sure she was still alive — Ilda was the exception, but she was considerably younger than Chaya, and Vashti preferred the mature company.

Chaya read to her, kept company with her when she did not want to talk, and listened when she did. Vashti had a bad habit of complaining, for hours, about Ahasuerus, and how she had never been given the chance to have a good marriage. At the end of such rants, Chaya would offer some wise tidbit, like "now she could focus on bringing up her child, instead of raising, in a sense, her husband," or "how now she was no longer married, she could take a breath and relax." Then Vashti would go on about the toils of a day while she was reigning and how taxing it was on her. After a while, Chaya stopped responding and simply listened while sewing or going about her household tasks.

Vashti continued to receive letters from the palace, and with each arrival, her mood would sour. It was a vicious cycle, where she would almost become content with living in the community of the Sisters, and then another letter from Haman's wife would arrive and it was back to missing her old life and how glorious the days were when she was the jewel of Ahasuerus' eye. How unfair it was that she was being replaced.

~*~*~*~

In the days before giving birth, Vashti's throat swelled shut three times, forcing her to stop talking and just listen. In doing so, her eyes began to open. Many times, Beanbean came in to change her sheets, only to find her staring out of the window, watching some of the "Daughters" laugh while washing clothes — her clothes. Zethar graciously found her a writing utensil and blank tablet, so she could at least write when she wanted to talk to someone.

The first thing she wrote was: *Beans, is it possible that any good could actually come out of being in this place?*

"If you want it to. I mean, this is the rest of your life. It would be heart-breaking to watch you waste away because you didn't want to see anything past 'not the palace'."

What do you do?

"Me?" Beanbean took a deep breath. "As a child, I liked writing little poems and songs to accompany my brother on the qanun. Sometimes I try to start writing music again."

I didn't know you had a brother, she wrote.

"That was a long time ago."

Instead of glossing over this, Vashti watched and noticed his demeanor change. She asked him for more and saw his face light up.

"He was my older brother," Beanbean began, "Father kept him as the heir and gave me to the imperial service. It was only right. I loved my brother, and we are quite close growing up. We served in the army together, when I served my tour against the Greeks. We were young men then. He had just married. We fought at Miletus, when we sacked the city. Only he never came home. He died shortly before the city fell," he pressed the tip of a finger against his neck, "hit by an arrow. It was fairly instantaneous, so he felt little pain and had no time for fear."

Vashti's brow furrowed. Beans gave it no mind and continued.

"Then we sacked the city, carried away its people as slaves and burned whatever plunder we couldn't carry. That's where I got these," he held up his scarred arm, "fighting the Greeks."

He may have meant to say more, but the door creaked open with a tap and Ilda slipped in quietly with a tray in her arms.

It was stacked with things for tea: leaves and spices, honey and ginger and cinnamon for soothing the throat, medicinal herbs for the head and the stomach.

As she crossed the room to the fireplace, she changed the cadence of her humming ever so slightly to acknowledge the two of them. Setting the tray down on a little table, Ilda glanced up at a map of the known world which had been drawn by men of a brother community. Beanbean and Vashti watched as Ilda put the kettle on the fire and began to prepare different mixtures for her lady. Her humming slowed as her eyes were drawn to the northeast, beyond the Hellespont and Thrace, past Macedonia and the farthest reaches of Greece. Her hands stilled, and she seemed lost in thought.

Vashti wrote on her tablet and handed it to Beanbean. He glanced at it, looked up at her, and then turned his eyes to Ilda. Looking back at his lady, he nodded and smiled in the corner of his mouth.

"Is that your home?" he asked.

Ilda startled and spun around. "Oh! I was wandering in my ... ingenuity."

"Imagination," suggested Beanbean, while laughter stuck in Vashti's swollen throat.

"Imagination," echoed Ilda. She glanced at Vashti's face, and seeing her eyes sparkling with attentiveness, answered the question. "I was thinking of home," she turned back to the map, making an effort to continue with the tea preparation while her mind and memory again wandered. The map showed India and hinted at the lands beyond it from whence came tin and spices; it showed the wild north-lands beyond Chorasmia and Sogdiana where the winters brought snow and the summers brought barbarians mounted on stout ponies; it showed the lands beyond the deserts of Arabia from whence came gold; it showed the farthest limits of Libya; it showed all the territory of the Greeks, and beyond that, blank space until the margins of the map.

"Tell me about it," questioned Beanbean for Vashti, "how did you come to be in Persia?"

"My tribe dwelt near the rivers between the mountains and the sea. One day an eastern tribe attacked, and I was taken by them. They took me east, and south, and then gave me to another tribe, who took me east and further south. They took me over the mountains, and I was traded from tribe to tribe until I came to Greece, where I was bought as a slave. Then I was taken across the sea to Miletus, and sold again." She paused briefly and continued dejectedly, "I was in Miletus when the Persians attacked."

Vashti's eyes darted to Beanbean, and Beanbean's to hers.

"They destroyed the Miletians, who were the closest thing I'd had to a people since being taken from my home. My master was good, and his household was my tribe. I watched them kill the men, and sell the women as slaves, and make all the boys eunuchs to serve the satraps. Then they took us all away. I was marched down the King's Highway with the other women; and when we reached Susa, I was the last one left, the others all having been sold in Asia and Mesopotamia. So they sold me to the royal palace."

Vashti turned to look at Beanbean again — just in time to see him slip silently out of the door. She was still surprised by his ability to do that. Glancing back at Ilda, she was relieved to see that the girl was completely ignorant of his absquatulation. Ilda shook her head and returned to preparing tea. The water was boiling now.

"But today, this is my tribe," she said, pouring the water over a concoction, "you and the children and the Daughters of Jephthah." She brought the tea over to Vashti. "Give it a moment to steep and cool down," she said, setting the cup down and pressing a hand gently to her lady's forehead. "Is the pain very bad?"

Vashti smiled and shook her head. It was not so bad.

The real pain came when it was time for the baby to be born. The Sisters had jumped into action, aiding her in any way they could to keep her alive. It was almost as bad as her labor with Nastaran, when she had almost died. But, just like when she birthed Nastaran, Beanbean was right there beside her, along with Ilda and Chaya. Vashti labored for days, but she could feel life bursting forth from this place. healthy and beautiful, pink and squirming and wailing, Vashti started to see the color, instead of choosing to see gray desolation. She saw the smiles of the Sisters and tasted the food with the flavor of love and care.

"Do you have a name for her, Majesty?" Zethar held the child while Vashti rested.

"Rana. She will be a living representation of my old life and my new life. The beauty of the old life I found in money and power, but it's different here. It's different. It's...real." Rana, from birth, was to be a village child, cared for everyone as if she were their shield.

Vashti slept for six days after this. "Labor is exhausting," Beanbean whispered to an anxious Ilda, "let her rest."

~*~*~*~

A year passed with a constant flow of letters, all of which relayed the details of how the selection of a new queen was proceeding, and constantly updated Vashti on the school progress of her older children.

"My lady," Chaya scurried in, breathing heavily, with the letters of the week. "She's been chosen. The new Queen of Persia."

"Well. Who is it?" Vashti questioned, as she nursed her newborn baby, a task she had never seen all the way through, since the palace had wet nurses available in her previous life. Having become bored with the mundane task, she was eager to find out who would be the chosen replacement.

Chaya began to answer, but Vashti stopped her. "Wait." Rana was finished eating, so instead of burping her daughter on her shoulder, she sat and waited while

Ilda anxiously heated up a pot of tea. She smoothed her tan skirts and placed her hands on her lap.

"Okay. I'm ready. Who is she?"

"Her name is Esther."

Vashti nodded and gently patted Rana's back. The sleepy baby gurgled and put a fist in her mouth.

"She is from Persia."

"Yes… and? Who is her family? How old is she?"

"Fifteen."

Vashti paused, eyebrows raised slightly. "Fif…teen?"

"And her family is… Unknown. We think she's an orphan."

In the midst of her peaceful new life, Vashti felt as if her world was again knocked off its kilter. She began seeing red.

"She's…"

"Fifteen and unknown. Yes." Chaya laughed nervously and started edging backwards, slowly.

Tarshin and Zethar walked in at the same time, but all they heard was "fifteen and unknown." Their Queen's face revealed the whole situation though.

"She needs to go outside," Tarshin whispered to Zethar as Beanbean called down the hallway, "Does anyone have an ax I can borrow?"

The next thing you need to know about this situation is that first, Vashti ran outside of her own volition; and second, the tree was not supposed to fall that hard.

The succession of people running down the hill across the field to the woods went as follows: Vashti tripping over her skirts because she was too angry to gather them up and did not care whether they tore, followed by Zethar carrying an ax, Beanbean carrying baby Rana, Ilda in a dither and a quandary, and Chaya with the letters.

"Read it again."

Zethar avoided eye contact as Vashti reached for the ax he was holding. She had grown quite a lot in this year of exile, to the point where she could lift a heavy ax and slam it into the thick trunk of a tree.

"What does the letter say, Chaya?" she repeated.

"Zeresh to Vashti, former Queen of Persia."

She heaved the ax into the tree, "FORMER queen?"

"I say former Queen," Chaya continued reading, "because a new Queen has been chosen. You'd hate her. She's young, I'd say about fifteen maybe, but no one really knows. Ahasuerus likes her because she's really something to look at, and — you'll love this part — she's an orphan. She doesn't have any known family at all. The palace records can't even find her birth."

Vashti hacked at the tree, again and again raising the ax and striking it down forcefully until the tree started to tilt. She kept hacking until the trunk started to give way.

"Queen Vashti!" Zethar jumped, pushing the Queen out of the way as the tree fell hard on the ground, the sound echoing through the forest and ricocheting off the compound walls further up the slope. For a moment, everyone stared silently at the tree … until Rana started to cry.

"It's fine." Beanbean yielded to a sudden compulsion to redirect the situation in response to the Queen's eyes welling up with tears. "We can have a fire tonight. And serve dinner outside. It would be good for us, urge the people to get outside a little more. And the weather is perfect for it. Don't you think, *Zethar*?"

Beanbean's eyes bulged as he looked back and forth between Zethar and Chaya. Chaya slowly rolled the letter back up and slid it into the cylinder.

"This should go in the fire tonight," she whispered.

"Now that is an excellent idea," Zethar said quickly, "I agree wholeheartedly with Chaya."

The journey back to the commune was far less dramatic. Vashti lost all of her energy and crumbled to the ground, refusing to move on her own. Walking back, Chaya carried baby Rana, who was fed by a nursemaid from amount Jephtha's daughters and immediately fell asleep, while Zethar and Beanbean carried Vashti. Ilda followed up the procession, gingerly carrying the letter from Zeresh.

That night at the bonfire, Vashti sobbed, grieving the loss of her former life. Rumors had spread that Ahasuerus was actually in love with his new bride. Even as she held his baby, it sickened her to hear from so many people that he was in love with someone else. At one time, she had been convinced that he was in love with her.

Beanbean comforted her the whole time, letting her cry on his arm, willingly taking turns holding the baby, and trying to coax her to eat something. Occasionally, he balanced Rana in his arms while she tried to stand on her own.

For the next three days, she did not eat anything and Rana cried incessantly.

"It will become easier with time." Beanbean soothed.

"I hate your advice," Vashti spat her words at him because she did not want it to be true. The royal part of her still wanted her husband to come and save her from this prison he had put her in, but she knew that was never going to happen. And in time, as Beanbean said, things did get easier.

In time.

Part 5

A month passed, and Vashti began to feel a sense of peace, or at least a calming of the storm within her, which was quite a feat. But the calm was broken again by a letter from the palace. Or rather, the condition of the letter.

Vashti cast a concerned eye over the letter. Since the day it arrived, she agonized over it. It was a letter from her eldest son Arash, detailing his plot to overtake the throne from his father, Ahasuerus. He wrote that Bigthan and Teresh were aiding him, and would personally lay hands on the King and kill him; then Arash would step into the vacuum of power and claim the imperial throne of Persia. As he told it, the plot was fool-proof, but it was the condition of the envelope that disturbed Vashti. The canister showed signs, albeit well-hidden signs, of tampering. The seal was ever so slightly off — as if it had been broken and the letter opened — over the seam, the wax was stretched and smudged, and the signet impression appeared to have been redrawn in part by hand.

Had someone opened the letter? What did they know, and what would happen now? To Arash, to her? She hesitated to tell even Beanbean what was happening — if those who sat in the king's gate were opening private mail with impunity, who could be trusted?

Suddenly there was a clatter of hooves outside, and a multitude of raised voices. Someone shouted. Gates slammed. Presently, the sound of boots clipping swiftly and deliberately echoed down the hall, and a moment later the door swung open and slammed into the wall. Vashti gasped in surprise.

There stood Arash, his face red from either exertion or emotion, dust on his cloak and sand caked onto his boots. He stood, panting, one arm still holding the door open, staring at his mother. Vashti stared back in shock, half turned around in her chair. He looked so much older, so different than when she had left him. Neither said

Part 5.

a word. Voices rose in the wind from the courtyard below.

"Arash!" Vashti began, rising to her feet.

"Haman uncovered our plot!" Arash now rushed into the room, not pausing to shut the door. "I haven't an idea how, but he caught wind of it and upon investigation, exposed Bigthan and Teresh. I barely escaped with my life!"

Vashti's mind was reeling, but Arash's agitated state was not helping her understand. She realized that she needed to calm him and get the full story.

"Arash, sooth!" she commanded, "How did this happen? Tell me everything, slowly, in as much detail as you know, from beginning to end."

"Everything was perfectly fine, until I sent you my letter," Arash began again. "After that, things unraveled." Vashti sighed. So the letter had been opened! "After that, Carcas joined our conspiracy. Bigthan trusted him. But he was a spy and an informant, and he told Haman everything, and exposed everyone involved. But how specifically Haman caught on, I have no idea. Regardless, Bigthan and Teresh have been raised up on poles by now, and all their men beheaded."

"How did you escape, my son?"

"It was that Babylonian eunuch, Mardukaya. He came to me and told me the plot was undone, and suggested I escape while I could — and never return. Bigthan and Teresh were the only ones who knew I was commander of our conspiracy — they would never betray me. And Nastaran — Nastaran is safe! So when Mardukaya told me they were exposed, but assured me no one knew you or I were involved, I quickly gathered my men and rode here. So I have chosen exile. Were I to return, he told me, he would not be able to protect me."

"Mordecai," echoed Vashti, "he must have been the one who read the letter."

"Who did what?"

"Arash, are you as near-sighted as your father?!? Mordecai read your letter and uncovered your plot. He must have told someone, and they told the king. The King set Haman to investigate — but you are fortunate that he did not expose the two of us." Vashti wrung her wrists, trying to think quickly amidst a flood of realization and piece it all together.

"Mardukaya betrayed us!" spat Arash.

"No!" Vashti nearly shouted, "Mordecai had compassion on a stupid boy and saved not only his life, but also the life of his mother from his own folly. You have likely lost your throne forever, but you are far enough from your father that at least you will live beyond your next birthday. Remember, Mordecai is from Babylon. I am from Elam. Our people may never have been friends, but we both hated the Persians. You were lucky that a friend like this discovered you, and not some currish Mede. He was both loyal to his King and kind to his neighbor. Without that happy turn of chance, you would be on top of a gibbet right now."

Arash cast his eyes down at the floor. Vashti waited for him to speak. He closed his eyes, took several deep breaths, and then looked back up at her. "I am chastened and bowed," he said, sarcasm mixed with genuine submission and assent. Vashti could not really be upset with him, but he needed one last reminder of his presumption and error.

"Do not forget, my son, that your plot would have left the throne of Persia to me, until you came of age. You have cost me much by your carelessness. And never forget, that while Mordecai may have let you live out of his compassion, I brought you into this world and I can take you out of it. I birthed you without a beard, and I may well bury you without one."

Fear and anger flashed across Arash's eyes, but then he turned without a word and left the room, his boots clipping back down the passageway. Vashti looked around her at the bare walls and bare floors.

The loneliness welcomed her to dwell in her permanent prison. She snatched Arash's letter off the table and cast it into the fire. There was no point anymore — the best it could do now was incriminate her and her son.

~*~*~*~

In the months that followed, Arash sat with his mother, many times, watching the sun rise. He told her about all of the palace happenings since her departure. He had to assure her early on that none of his siblings were in danger from his failed schemings. He told her how Bahar, now ten years of age, was training to be a soldier — since his mother had fallen from favor, he had no prospects upon the merit of his birth alone even with his own father and especially not in his father's court, and so he was set to seek his fortune upon the field of battle, maybe one day becoming a general. He told her of Ayena's adjusting well and finding friendship and safety among the other members of the King's household. It saddened Vashti's heart when he confessed to her that little Ayena hardly remembered her. But mostly he told her about Nastaran, how selecting a husband for her had gone, about Nastaran's engagement portrait and marriage, the selection of a new queen and his father's second marriage — and the second selection of concubines.

"If he had done that to me, he wouldn't reign another year. I would have assassinated him myself."

"It was a bad situation to be in, for her. I wouldn't have known what to do either. I almost felt bad for her."

Vashti rolled her eyes. "Felt bad for her? She's just a child."

"Exactly. This is her first marriage. It's a situation worthy of pity."

"Nonsense. You are in a situation worthy of pity."

"Mama!"

Rana jumped around the corner, stopped when she saw Arash and displayed her perfect forward roll, which landed her at his feet. She playfully gazed up at him and extended her arms, like she wanted him to hold her. And he did. "My sister seems to be very well, which I'm pleased to see."

"Pick me up, Arash!"

Arash leapt to his feet and scooped his sister up. She squealed with glee and wiggled in his arms.

They spoke to each other in little sing-song voices. Little Rana's eyes soaked up everything she could about him, touching his face like she was trying to memorize it. Arash laughed and it reminded Vashti, with a pang of remorse, of when he was a child. Those years would never come back, but new ones would be here to cherish. So she let herself breathe and relish the moment.

~*~*~*~

A few weeks later, a letter arrived from a palace, but not the one in Babylon. The seal was different. Vashti was quickly growing tired of letters, but opened it nonetheless. The handwriting at the beginning was unfamiliar, but something that smelled vaguely sweet wafted from the inside. She tapped out the scroll and a sprig of rosemary and a small vine of ivy fell out onto her hand. Her heart beat as fast as the scurry of children's feet, and her hands shook as she unrolled it.

"Queen Vashti. From Lady Nastaran, in the year" blah blah blah. That part is completely unimportant. Vashti impatiently scanned it until she found the meat of the letter.

Mama,

I hope this letter makes it to you safely, and that you are well. I know Arash is with you now, but unfortunately I have to tell you, as I am ashamed to say, I am partially responsible for the plot to kill father. It was only after years of asking questions and my finally being married off for me to find out why you were sent away. I believe it was incredibly immature and quite vile for father to demand so much from you and then to give such harsh consequences. It was cruel. After discovering this, I spoke with Arash and we thought him unfit to be king, and decided to take matters into our own hands instead of waiting and watching like you taught us. I could have successfully dethroned father and Arash could have been King, but we were hasty and trusted the wrong people. It was a mercy that he wasn't killed for his part in it. I'm sorry I put my brother's safety in jeopardy because of my own anger. I promised I would not forget you and that I would protect them. I suppose that I thought protecting the city would protect Arash, but I was also fueled by anger.

I made sure Ayena and Bahar were in good hands before I left. I had wanted to secret them to you long ago, but it was too risky — father's philosophy seems to be "Keep your friends close and your enemies closer." Why he's more worried about Bahar than Arash, I don't know. Or maybe, mother, he actually likes Bahar, and that's why he's having him trained in military leadership. He's also arranging a marriage for Ayena, but I have already been asking him to let her come live with me. With the new "queen" luckily, Ayena has less value in the eyes of ambitious noblemen — that, considered with how busy father is now with his own concerns, leaves me in good hope that he will relent and send her to me.

All that you have taught me in the past has paid off tenfold. I have become the lady of a regent in Armenia. It's a land with beautiful sloping hills and air a little more chilly than the cities of Persia, but it's beautiful. I love it here. And I have started cultivating gardens, which of course, are dedicated to you. I have been married 3 years and have successfully given my husband two children. The loves of my life. Azadah and Zal are dearer to me than my own heart. Azadah came first, though, and it caused us a scare. All is well though, because Zal is healthy and has just started walking. I'm carrying my third baby now.

Azadah likes being in the gardens as much as I did when I was young. I gave her a crown of eucalyptus instead of rosemary. She likes drawing, so she drew something for you. I'm happy, mama. I know you're alive and well, I know Arash is stupid but still living, and my baby siblings are growing big. I wish you could be here to see my gardens. They're Persia-inspired, just like the flowing gardens at home.

Mama, you were always a treasure even when you were not recognized as one. I hope that in your new life, you find the peace you deserve.

Forever your daughter,
Nastaran

Letters from Nastaran were always the best part of any day, any week, even. Her daughter's words rang true and comforting. Finally, breathing came easier.

Part 6

The plot had failed and life went on. Went on for four years! Rana grew tall like her brothers and sisters. No evil befell them on account of her son's scheme, and eventually Vashti ceased to worry. Arash also forgot about his embarrassment and failure, working in the community with the eunuchs. He had to live in the village, away from the Daughters of Jephthah, but he could visit during the day. He worked alongside his mother — there was much work to be done. Staying busy kept Vashti's spirits up.

Frequently, Vashti paced the hallways in thought, but on this day, she was contemplating how to improve the gardens. For a couple years she had been playing with the idea of a fountain — or two or three! She made it all the way to the kitchens before stopping dead in her tracks. In the recent weeks, every letter was delivered by one boy, not bad looking, and he seemed to have a little bit of a crush on Chaya. That one delivery boy who fancied Chaya, stood now at the door. Chaya was facing him, but she appeared burdened with something. Her shoulders were hunched and the hushed conversation caught Vashti's attention. She stopped moving, to better hear, but the boy stopped talking and left hastily, after squeezing Chaya's shoulder.

Ooh. Vashti thought to herself. *Our girl could have something of a romance afloat.*

"What was that all about?" Vashti picked up an apple on the counter, taking a huge bite out of it. She raised her eyebrows, looking out the door to watch him walk away.

Chaya wiped her face hastily but her eyes were still red. She looked at Vashti with big tear-stained, brown eyes. "There was a new decree from the palace."

"Okay?"

"Vashti," Chaya took both of her hands, leading her to a chair to sit. "this may come as a surprise to you, but..." She looked around, to see if anyone else was around. "You know how I pray without idols?"

"Yes…"

"And how I don't work on Saturdays?"

"Yes. It's because you were raised as a Daughter of Jephthah."

She hesitated. "Partially. It's because… I'm also Jewish."

"Oh." Vashti paused.

"I believe there is only one God."

Vashti's mouth fell open. "You…are? Oh."

"The palace just decreed that the Jews are to be killed on the Thirteenth of Adar. All of us."

"Oh." Vashti's stomach dropped. This had never happened to her before. She had been raised to be a Queen, and to leave the genocides and wars to the King. Her mind easily comprehended and understood the strategies of war, but to actually be on the receiving end of a genocidal attack … Vashti hated to even think about it. But she was no longer a Queen. She was the King's ex-wife, living in exile, hundreds of miles away from the city. In reality, this was her home now and these were her people. It only took nine years for her to realize and accept it.

"Everyone here is Jewish, aren't they?"

"Not everyone." Chaya started to shake, and her breaths became more shallow. "But yes, most of us."

"Who is going to carry out the King's order?" She asked, even though she did not want to know the answer. The royal part of her already knew. The new side of her — the side that was slowly growing to care for others — wished Chaya would not say what she expected. It took a minute, but Chaya finally answered.

"His citizens."

Part 7

As soon as the edict was announced, life inside the compound felt as if it had been sucked out. The entire community immediately went into mourning. Including the Sisters who were not Jewish, everyone wore sullen black and kept their faces covered. The usually joyful atmosphere of lively music turned somber and every one cried out to their god to save them.

A letter arrived from the palace, but it was not for Vashti. Everyone gathered in the largest hall as it was read aloud.

"Queen Esther is going to appear before the King in three days. She wants us to pray and fast, that the King may find favor with her and grant her request."

"What is her request?" Ilda listened, edging closer and closer to the middle of the circle.

"She's going to try to save us."

A series of gasps went through the group. Across the room, Vashti saw Chaya drop to her knees, clasp her hands together, and start whispering prayers to her God. Soon, others followed.

The next three days were a whirlwind of prayer and fasting. No one ate, barely anyone spoke. This was the first time Vashti could say she felt that the compound was truly a home. The Jewesses followed such a joyous God that made them so happy, moments like this were scarce, but the feeling was not sequestered to just them. Vashti's children and servants observed all of the happenings around them, and she could see in their behavior, the curiosity that influenced them. Sometimes, Arash would skip meals, instead sitting outside watching a group of the Daughters of Jephthah pray. Sometimes he would leave to take walks with some of the Jewish men from the nearby town. Ilda started singing the Jewish praises while doing housework and taking care of the baby. They did not seem to miss their Persian idols at all. To their credit, they had assimilated well, and now embraced their new community and culture.

The oncoming dark cloud of genocide plagued Vashti's thoughts. What would happen to her and her children? Where would they go? They were no longer under the palace's protection. Their only ties to security were Beanbean and Zethar.

Little Rana only knew this place. She had learned to walk, bracing herself against the stone walls, and when she fell, Zethar was almost always there to catch her. She had grown up here among the sisters. It made Vashti's heart warm, because though she had been a mother for eighteen years, she was only just becoming accustomed to her children in a sincere way.

When the three days of fasting ended, the entire commune seemed to hold its breath, waiting for a messenger to come up the road with news.

Part 8

News was scarce though. Vashti wearied at the thought of more useless letters from old friends in Susa, until the proclamation came out. Now she was hungry for some kind of news — even though it seemed all they ever brought was bad news. Even bad news would change the dynamic at the compound. Finally, one arrived. It sat on the table for an hour before she dared touch it. It obviously came from her old friend at Susa, Zeresh, the unfortunate wife of Haman, that cad. Up until now, Zeresh's letters had failed to excite her, and only left her with a vague feeling of dread and a weight of resignation hanging from her heart. She picked up the cylinder, broke the seal, shook the rolled up scroll out, and spread it across the table. It was long.

It began with the usual opening: "Zeresh, etc, to Vashti, etc, Greetings …" Mercifully, most of the actual formalities were skipped, and the usual courtly usage replaced with a facetious parody of the styles that centered on her and Zeresh's friendship and their equally miserable states: Vashti divorced and exiled from a husband she could neither forgive nor let go of, and Zeresh married to that king's right-hand squirrel.

Zeresh asked polite and genuine, but exceedingly annoying, questions, about how Vashti was faring and the welfare of her children — questions that had to be asked, and which Vashti would not have minded as much, if she had not already been in a poor mood. Zeresh then talked about herself and her family, rendering an update on each of her ten sons and Dasha her daughter. She started in on affairs of the court and the empire, and Vashti started glossing over the words. Another useless letter? Zeresh might humor her with some information about what was going on outside of the narrow world of the Daughters of Jephthah. Then something arrested her eyes. A name. The name of Esther. How had that brat wiggled her way into Vashti's letters!

She was already in Vashti's palace and robes and role and crown — could she leave the rest of her life alone? But what was it Zeresh wanted to say about her? Maybe this Babylonian snippet had contracted some fatal disease from an Indian servant.

Haman has been invited to a second banquet with the great King hosted by Esther, and has been out all day. I know you don't care to hear her name, but this is important, Vashti, and a rather interesting story. Yesterday she entered Ahasuerus' presence uninvited. I wasn't there, so I don't know quite what happened, but you know what sort of a man, to use the term loosely perhaps, your husband is, and it surprised me to hear he did not hesitate to hold out his scepter to her — I was expecting her head to roll, quite frankly. Last time someone approached uninvited, Cyrus the Pretender lost his life — you will forgive the tasteless humor, but I had high hopes for this incident. Well, there is great speculation as to why she has come before the king, with her charm turned up, best gown on, fresh-faced and pulling all the usual stops. She clearly wanted something, one should think. And you know Ahasuerus. If he's not busy killing someone, he's using them somehow. And he likes pretty things. So he was taken like a deer in the snare, waiting to take an arrow to the liver. He hastened like a bird into her net, offering her anything she wanted — just to look at her! Vashti, the little girl has wrapped this man around her little finger like he was a daisy! Stiff-necked Ahasuerus is like an Indian dancer suddenly. So gentle and kind, affectionate and attentive with her. Yet what does she have that you never did? Impertinence is what. If Ahasuerus likes imps like this, let him class himself below us.

Vashti did not quite see it that way. She had spent years of marriage trying to break Ahasuerus of his bad habits and character flaws and reshape him into his potential and her ideal — and Zeresh was making it sound like Esther had done just that with completely opposite tactics. What Vashti would not have given to have Ahasuerus wrapped around her little finger!

But anyway, back to the story: all she asks for is that the King and Haman attend a banquet that very day. Now, of course this was an impressive banquet - seven courses and then drinks over a game or two and some conversation. Ahasuerus and Haman figured she was buttering the King up for some other request, which I agree with — so Ahasuerus asked again, offering her anything she wanted. I would have asked for Maka and Gedrosia — the Greek problem being what it is, the trade routes of tin from

Part 8.   103

Siam will be extremely valuable in coming years. But all Esther asked for, again, was that King and Haman come to another of her banquets!

And Vashti, the strangest thing is that Haman has been invited to come before this girl, like being summoned to see the King — she is, after all, the Queen. Eunuchs aren't always allowed access to her if they are not specifically assigned or sent to her. But here is Haman, my husband, feasting privately with the great King and his Queen. He may be a squirrel, but there is something to be said, you know, for being married to the second most powerful man in the world. I may yet be able to ask for the ports of Maka and Gedrosia myself, ha-ha! Vashti, things are looking very promising for my sons' futures, and for Dasha, and perhaps my husband and I could use our position to help you too.

See, the way we figure it, Haman has been invited to these banquets because Esther's request has something to do with him. We don't know what it could be, but it should be big. Haman has high aspirations, and is hanging in anticipation to every word she says, hoping to catch a hint of what she might have planned. I've never seen him so excited. He's almost normal and enjoyable like this.

Only, one of the eunuchs has been bothering him — Mordecai, the Jew. Haman left the banquet yesterday in adulation and exultation, until he met Mordecai at the gate. The Jew has refused to bow to him or show him any respect for years, Vashti, and they hate each other. Then yesterday, as Haman is riding out the gate, perfectly willing to forgive Mordecai for all this and be the better man, there the Jew is, bowing and saying 'Have a good evening, sir,' with all the others like nothing ever happened and nary an apology for all the disrespect and causeless dislike. So of course Haman was furious, and came home in a stew — sometimes I do wish I'd married a butcher or a plumber or someone whose job was less stressful so I could have a quiet, peaceful home here. We stayed up all night, after he gathered his friends and confidants and counselors from around the city, talking about his status and his goals and aspirations and all and how well things were going for him with the King and Queen, and talking about how nice it would be if they could give him a raise. Then we stayed up longer talking about Mordecai the Jew and their years-long struggle and how greatly Mordecai had disrespected him and vexed him.

  Men are the worst, Vashti. You go to them and just want to talk about something to process through it and have an understanding and sympathetic friend, and they offer all sorts of stupid and unrealizable solutions without being asked to do so — but then when they have a problem of their own, twenty of them in a room together can't — in eight hours! — figure out a very simple problem. And that, I suppose, sums up government. But I digress. So Haman is in a stew *again because of Mordecai, and I say, "Why not build an execution stake here on the ground. Go to the King and get him to sign a warrant against Mordecai, and execute the Jew yourself tomorrow before your second banquet." "How?" he asks me. "You are the man in charge of investigating and thwarting assassinations and rebellions," I answered, "figure it out." The density of a male skull — we really have our work cut out for us, don't we?*

Vashti laughed aloud. She was enjoying herself with Zeresh's analysis of the male psyche. And she had been reluctant to read this letter! Though, what was it with Susa and killing Jews? Who started this whole trend? Really, it was not like they were Scythians or barbarians from beyond Chorasmia. These were citizens of the Persian empire! But the letter continued.

So he set out to do that, but while they were building the pole and platform by torchlight, I went to bed. Which, of course, was my plan the whole while! I expected to see a bit of kosher shish-kebab this morning when I got up, but the stake is empty, and Haman has been out all day, so I guess he will get to it tomorrow. But anyway, that is what Haman has been up to...

The letter went on for a little longer. But now Vashti noticed that near the top of the second page the hand changed. Zeresh had written in haste, and by the looks of it a certain level of distress.

PART 9

Oh Vashti, it's a disaster!

That sounded bad.

This whole time Esther was a Jew!

What was it with these people and Jews?!? Maybe she had gotten out at just the right time. The capital was going stir crazy over Jews, of all people.

Haman has fallen victim to his own enemies! I saw it coming though. He came home just before the second feast — as a matter of fact, he was almost late for it — and turns out he spent the whole morning, not executing Mordecai, but leading him in a parade to that Jew's honor, walking before him while this eunuch was mounted on the king's horse in the king's robe and decorated with royal paraphernalia, proclaiming to the whole city, "Thus shall it be done for the man whom the King desires to honor. All of Persia is Ahasuerus' bodyguard, but none more than this man, brave as a lion and as mighty as a thousand Immortal warriors. There is none the King delights in more among the men who serve him, nor is there a face like the face of this man, which stands before the face of the King with dignity and respect, seeing the King himself face to face." But it gets worse. He came home in a darker mood than he did last night, and he told all that had happened. Then I thought of all that was going on, with the edict against the Jews and a hundred other things that are going on here is Susa, Vashti, and I realized, if Mordecai, a Jew, is elevated above the King's own right hand when they are supposed to be summarily killed at the king's order as given by his right hand, then that right hand is in great danger of being cut off. I told him as much, and begged him to be careful, to be shrewd, and when the King's eunuchs came, with Harbonah, to call Haman to the banquet, I warned him not to go. But Haman was convinced the King and Queen were his closest friends, and he hurried away. And what did I tell him, but he is home again — impaled upon the very pole he thought to hang Mordecai from! Oh Vashti, what am I to do?!? I am sending Dasha away to Aria to stay with family until all of this is over. Word is Haman assaulted the Queen when he was *exposed. Of all the bone-headed things to do — but will I be implicated in this whole plot? He is being accused of conspiring to kill the Queen along with all the Jews! And I suggested the stake for Mordecai! Susa is no longer safe — chaos is about to break out like a disease, and anyone not aligned with the Jews shall die!*

Vashti stopped reading and set the letter down. So now the edict concerning the Jews made more sense. Haman and Mordecai had been feuding and Haman hated him so much he decided to abuse his office to kill not just this eunuch but an entire race of people — these poor people, who had been scattered to the four winds at the destruction of Jerusalem. She arose and began to pace.

She had always wondered about Mordecai. It made sense that he was a Jew — he kept aloof from everyone else in the citadel. He must have been right there when Esther was preparing to become Queen.

In an instant, all became clear. Dagon be fallen! Mordecai and Esther! He intercepted the letter from Arash, and passed it on to Esther, his fellow Jew. She informed the king, and he set Haman on the task of uncovering the plot, and Haman foiled Bigthan and Teresh's plot. Then in the end, Ahasuerus treated his new wife the way he had with a second beauty pageant for concubines (as if he did not have enough) and a cold shoulder. He really was a terrible husband, was he not?

So the Jews were the best thing that had ever happened to Ahasuerus, and Haman orchestrated to annihilate them for his own personal gain and defraud the crown while doing it — Vashti knew how these things worked: she had witnessed the siege of Babylon. When Mordecai got wind of this plot, and told the young Queen, the quick-witted girl devised and beautifully executed a plan to win Ahasuerus' favor. She had wooed him into helping her, saving her people and executing Haman, all the while playing Haman like a zither to the tune of his own hubris and a spectacular fall from favor ending in a brutal execution. He was probably still up there on that pole. Vashti shuddered to think that Zeresh was trapped in her house listening to her husband scream his death agonies.

Her mind was swirling. What did this all mean? She sat down and held her head in her hands. It would be a pickle, getting out of the unbreakable decrees of the Medes and the Persians, laws which bound even the King — but these clever Jews, Mordecai and Esther, probably already had a plan.

Part 10

Decrees were the most troublesome, anxious things Ahasuerus could possibly come up with, but still he kept sending them out.

This one was good news, though. Another decree from the palace concerning the Jews, but Mordecai's this time. The man who saved her son deserved to be in leadership. And now she was seeing and hearing the fruit of that.

The King's edict grants the Jews in every city the right to assemble and protect themselves; to destroy, kill and annihilate the armed men of any nationality or province who might attack them and their women and children, and to plunder their possessions.

So, the Jews were now allowed and encouraged to protect themselves. The fear that had been planted was immediately uprooted and replaced with hope and vengeance. The King was going to provide weapons of war to preserve them.

And it was not hidden who the attackers would be. The King was unable to retract a decree, the first one, where he enabled the hate. The ones who were originally sent to carry it out in the first place had already hardened their hearts and there was no going back from it. Arash, the Queen's son, was a man now, and remembered the training he received as a child. He went with the Jewish men into the nearby town, and spent weeks teaching them how to protect themselves. The King's weapons arrived by night at the compound, and were distributed in the morning.

~*~*~*~

Adonai yimloch l'olam vaed,
Adonai yimloch l'olam vaed.
The Lord God's reign will never end,

Adonai yimloch l'olam vaed.

~*~*~*~

Vashti was unrecognizable as a queen. In an apron and an old dress she bustled around moving supplies and tending to the frightened and huddled crowds seeking refuge within the compound walls. The compound became a fortress to protect the village women and children. The houses were set up as decoys. If the anti-Semites went to the houses, they would be met with a slew of traps. Within the walls of the compound,provisions were made, as the guests would need places to sleep, and food to eat. Vashti went from room to room, making sure they had enough space for everyone.

The night before, the compound rested in a hush. Everyone waited, poised in anxious anticipation and engulfed by silence. Even the children felt the somber presence everyone was experiencing. And the sun still rose. And with it, war, but not as originally intended.

The end.

I lied, it's not the end.

Vashti watched from a high window as dawn broke over the hilltops. She found herself praying to the God of the Jews that her son would be safe, then caught herself. When did this happen? It kind of felt natural at this point, with all she had seen, heard and felt, and even in her own life. Here in the frontier near the desert, there were not many men to rise against the Jews, but her heart still slightly feared them — she was mostly worried for her son's safety. That was, until she saw the league of Jewish men confronting the men of the King. They were like a shield fortifying the compound. They charged forward and Vashti turned her face away, looking instead to her daughter, making tea for a mother and child whose father was out fighting. Rana was taking her name and manifesting it, becoming a true shining light at the commune.

As soon as the work had been done, Rana ran outside into the gardens, where she found solace. She recharged as soon as she stepped into the sunlight. Her daughter was the living manifestation of a peaceful and content life. This girl had never known the busy, high life of the palace, but all of her joy was fresh and new. Even now, as she begged her mother to write down every plant that she knew, she bubbled over with joy.

"Mama, it's important to write down what you know so the information can live longer." She had explained when she bound her new journal. "Isn't it exciting, mama?" She eagerly went on about how it would be such an amazing experience to write her own book of remedies and how that could heal and affect so many people. Of course she said yes, because Rana's joy was quickly becoming her weakness.

She was surprised to find herself content and at peace, giving all of her knowledge to her ten year old daughter. She barely thought of Ahasuerus anymore, although Nastaran was constantly on her mind. Rana had begun to look more and more like her father. She had his nose, but growing up, the girl's face was a mirror image of her mother and older sisters. It made her sad some days, still heartbroken over her lost children, but Rana was such a gift that the sadness could not linger.

Vashti dug her hands in the dirt, two days after the anti-semite purge, while her daughter questioned all of her plant knowledge. She was renovating the gardens so the flowers could bloom in time for the heat of the summer.

"What about rosemary?" She plucked some from the vine. "It's a little oily and has a distinctive smell." She mused, rolling it between her fingers.

"Rosemary is good for healing the mind. Back when I was living at home, my older sister fell and hit her head really hard. The impact was so hard that she looked me in the face and didn't know who I was, but her handmaidens laid her in rosemary for days until she began remembering things again."

Vashti laughed. "I was gone and married to your father before she was fully healed, but I received a letter from her years later saying she was well."

"That's fascinating." Rana started writing, then stopped, noticing a change in her mother's mood.

"You look like you have something else to say."

Vashti paused. "Nastaran."

"My older sister?"

"Yes. When she was little...," Vashti smiled with the memory rediscovered. "She was about four. We had watched her father put the crown on, because I thought it would be good for her to see the courts in action. Afterwards, I had a room in my quarters for the healing plants, and she pulled some rosemary out from the root to try and make a crown for herself because she thought it looked like the one her father wore. It didn't and she got upset about it. Then she cried, because she thought I was going to be upset about it." Her face softened, and her eyes absentmindedly fell to the ground. "I pulled some ivy from the balcony and made it into a better crown for her. And she fell asleep. The smell of herbs always coaxed her to sleep. Specifically mint leaves."

Vashti snapped out of her memories, which swirled in her head like a dance. "What smells do you like?"

Rana sat back and thought before answering. "I really like eucalyptus. It's soothing."

"Oh, eucalyptus has so many benefits. It's good for soothing and relaxing, yes, but do you know where eucalyptus comes from?..."

Back when she lived at the palace, Vashti had officiated the gardens under her command, but in her new home, there was all of this land, and only time and resources to garden vegetables. She was given a small plot of land to garden, right on the edge of the woods, to cultivate pretty flowers. The "healing garden," as they called it, not only held herbs, but it gave sick children a peaceful place to sit outside and admire the flowers, which itself seemed to heal them. Bahar, one of her only remaining children still living in the palace, had sent some seeds in a letter and she had set her mind to planting them. She thought of how the climate would affect their growth and how much she should nurture them so they would grow beautifully.

Rana left in search of something to eat, but came back hanging over Arash's shoulder. She was dangling, holding her "healing journal." Vashti watched as he dropped her on the ground and snatched the book out of her hands and ran with it, waving it over his head.

"Mama, make him give it back. The pressed leaves are going to fall out!" Rana whined, making her way to her feet and chasing after him. She caught up and grabbed onto his legs, making him hit the ground hard … right in the middle of the bed Vashti was cultivating.

"Ay!" She threw a wad of wet dirt at him. "When I was young we weren't allowed to be outside and play in the dirt like this. Don't misuse this earth we've been given." She hiked up her skirts and walked over to him, brushing the dirt from his hair and from his shoulders. "Now look. You're completely covered."

Rana got up and started brushing him off too. He smiled and leaned on her again, brushing a piece of hair out of her face.

"Thank you mother, but the least of my worries is a little dirt. I do care deeply for your gardens though. They are going to be beautiful."

Chaya walked with a young man close to the commune. When they looked up and saw Vashti and Arash, the young man waved, revealing his injured arm.

"That's the man I fought next to yesterday. He's a brave man."

"Didn't he used to bring our mail from the city?"

Arash shook his head. "He's the one who brought me safe passage from the palace." He looked back fondly. "I'm glad to call him my friend."

Vashti's heart swelled. She had never expected such kindness from a man she had only looked at as the mail carrier. She thought about the way things could have been, how differently the path of destiny could have run for them all. With only one misstep, her son could have been found out and hanged. He could have been killed on his journey. It was only by the grace of providence that he had lived to reach the commune those many years ago, and only by the same grace that he had survived the previous day's battle.

"I hope he's good to Chaya."

"I hope Chaya is good to him."

They watched him lean on her for support, walking slowly to the door. Chaya talked to him and led him quietly, not making too big of a fuss, but still fixing his bandages, which were loosening.

Eventually, as the sun started its descent in the west, Vashti cleaned up her garden tools and walked to one of the hills overlooking the commune. She moved to sit under a tree with her Rana, who was falling asleep fast. Vashti watched the sun set, until the stars came out, reflecting on her blessings. She had grown food that would feed her daughter, so she could grow up physically healthy and strong, but most importantly grow grateful for the sacrifice. Rana had successfully grown her first broccoli plant and they ate it a few nights before. The taste of it was even more magnificent, with the knowledge of the work that had gone into it. Even now, sitting under this orange tree, every aspect of her life felt like a blessing. Music flowed gently from the compound.

> Adonai yimloch l'olam vaed,
> Adonai yimloch l'olam vaed.
> The Lord God's reign will never end,
> Adonai yimloch l'olam vaed.

Vashti leaned her head back and joined their song, singing joyfully with relief,

> Though the sun may one day shine no more,
> Though the waves may stop their race to the shore,
> Though the birds of the air may no longer sing,
> Though the winter fail to be followed by spring,

> Adonai yimloch l'olam vaed,
> Adonai yimloch l'olam vaed.
> The Lord God's reign will never end,
> Adonai yimloch l'olam vaed.

She rose with Rana, took her hand and they started back down to the compound together.

While slaves in Egypt to Pharaoh's throne,
While crossing the desert in search of a home,
While always outnumbered by enemy men,
While cast out and longing to come home again,

When those who are foolish are said to be wise,
When love waxes cold and enemies rise,
When it seems as though you just can't go on,
When everything that there is is gone,

>Adonai yimloch l'olam vaed,
>Adonai yimloch l'olam vaed.
>The Lord God's reign will never end,
>Adonai yimloch l'olam vaed.

>Adonai yimloch l'olam vaed,
>Adonai yimloch l'olam vaed.
>The Lord God's reign will never end,
>Adonai yimloch l'olam vaed.

Along with the rest, Vashti and Rana and Arash, Chaya, Beanbean and Zethar, joined the chorus.

ENDING

The tune of the hymn lingered in his memory as he finished the last lines of the scroll. Why such a sad song at the end of a happy story? But then there was a lot to the story that he could not understand — so maybe it was a sad story too, blended with the happiness.

"Kibel."

The boy jumped up from where he had been sitting in the window and nearly dropped the scroll from his lap onto the floor.

"Uncle! I'm sorry — I didn't — I was just —"

"Relax, Kibel," his uncle smiled, as he sat near him on the bed. "I see you've found my surprise for Purim."

Kibel smiled sheepishly, still nervous that he had been caught reading his uncle's private papers.

"Did I ruin the surprise?"

"Not at all, my lad," his uncle rubbed his big, bald head, "I think I managed to surprise you anyway, did I not?" The big man let out a big laugh, and Kibel laughed too.

"But the surprise wasn't just for you, but for everyone, and," his uncle continued, "there is more to it."

"More to it?"

"You'll see, when it comes. Now, let's say we rejoin the party."

"Wait, uncle, I have a question."

"Yes?"

Now Kibel hesitated, trying to find the right words. "There is so much I don't understand ..."

"What sorts of things?"

"Well, some of what happens in the story. Their lives are so much different from our own. What does it mean, to put away your wife in divorce the way the King did? How could he take another wife besides the first? No one we know has ever had more than one wife ever ... and I've never heard the Purim story in this way before. I don't understand why ... how ..."

"You don't understand why I chose this Purim story over the one your rabbi loves? It doesn't seem to have that much to do with Purim, does it?"

Kibel, unsure whether to nod at the first or shake his head at the latter, shook it slowly.

His uncle nodded, but then there was a clatter from down below, and a cart rumbled into the courtyard. Kibel looked out the window with his uncle, and they watched a tall woman with long gray hair climb down from the cart with the help of young men who must have been her grandsons. Quite a number of people were down there now, milling about and flocking towards the door.

"How about we go down stairs," smiled the man. "I think more of the story will make sense."

Kibel followed his uncle downstairs, and they reached the door just as their new guests did. The tall gray-haired woman was there, embracing his mother.

"Chaya!" she exclaimed

"It is so good to see you!" replied his mother.

His uncle stepped up as the women released each other.

"Aren't you a little short to be Haman?" asked the woman.

A mischievous glint came to his uncle's eyes. "Aren't you a little old to be Queen Esther?"

"Old!?!" Playfully exclaimed the tall woman.

A slight woman with blonde hair and light eyes entered among the great crush of people coming in. "Ilda!" cried Kibel's mother, "I didn't know you were coming!"

"Vashti insisted on bringing me," grinned the other as they embraced.

Kibel looked at the tall gray-haired woman, who was now talking with his father and an older cousin, smiling broadly and holding one of the smaller children in her arms. *So this was Vashti?* She held herself with dignity, but aside from that she looked almost like any other Jewish grandmother. He started thinking about it, then shook his head in disbelief. Vashti in his uncle's house? How had Uncle Tarsh come to know the former Queen of Persia?

"Beanbean," said the tall woman turning, and suddenly Kibel realized: Uncle Tarsh was Beanbean. It all made sense now … kinda.

As the day went on and festivities stretched into the evening, Kibel watched Vashti. She played with the younger children, laughed along with everyone else, acted well the part of Queen Esther, listened carefully to everything that was said in conversation, talked softly of the dark days with the others, cheered their deliverance from Haman, and helped with everything: from food preparation and cleaning to taking care of spills and messy children. But nevertheless, the dignity she carried herself with did not elevate her above the household tasks of the day, but rather elevated the tasks themselves. This was queenly grace, true queenly grace in action. This was humility.

As the evening lingered, they all sat in a circle, the fire burning on the hearth, sharing what they had learned from the story of Esther and Mordecai.

"It is about providence," said Vashti, "about times when you don't understand why things are happening the way they are and nothing seems to be going right — when you are widowed or orphaned or taken from your home or left powerless and hurting — God is in control and He is working all things together for the good of those who love Him and are called according to His purpose. He is in control of the rising and falling of kings and queens, and has made us all for such a time as this: right now. We have to be faithful in this moment with what is immediately in front of us. We have to trust in Him and take responsibility as good stewards."

"Esther's story is about pride," Kibel piped up, "because trust and stewardship only come by humility: to believe in all Adonai has promised, and to obey Him. Mordecai's pride put the Jews in danger; Haman's pride cost him his life; Esther had to put aside self-love as well to go before the King, being obedient and faithful unto death perhaps." He pulled out his scroll of quotes from his father, and finding a specific one, he read carefully. "Contention comes by pride, but those who humble themselves, and pray and seek Adonai's face, and turn from ways of selfishness and pride, then He will hear from Heaven, and will forgive their sins and heal their lands." That's what it means."

"And Queen Vashti stumbled in her pride," said Vashti, "and only by humility learned the way of peace amidst all the storms of life." She winked at Kibel from across the room. "Thank you, Kibel. Thank you all for letting me celebrate our deliverance with you."

Special Thanks

Special thanks to Professor Colin Smith for teaching the class on the book of Esther, which inspired the creation of this book.

Thanks also to Kaylin Fischer and Molly Mayo for final stage edits, and Michaella Saccullo for writing the introduction.

Thanks are due also to Lily Kreiger, Madeline Kleveter, and Victor Baker for their art work. It is spectacular and we know the effort and time you put in amidst busy schedules, period, exclamation mark.

We would also like to thank both of our moms, Chiana Sanderson and Elizabeth Swift, for encouraging the pursuit of writing.

CPSIA information can be obtained
at www.ICGtesting.com
Printed in the USA
LVHW021300010523
745751LV00016B/1505